The Vegetable Patch

Written by Lynne Masson

Illustrated by Laura Sawyer

AuthorHouse™
1663 Liberty Drive
Bloomington, IN 47403
www.authorhouse.com
Phone: 1-800-839-8640

Published by AuthorHouse 10/29/2012

ISBN: 978-1-4772-3859-2 (sc)

authorHOUSE®

To Ciara
Best Wishes
Lynne Masson
December 2012
18/100

3

THE VEGETABLE PATCH

Farmer Betteridge had a very large farm with lots of animals, fields for them to graze in and other fields full of wheat and barley.

He also had a very large garden at the back of his cottage which had lots of flowers, a lawn, a play area for the children Molly and Jack, and a large vegetable patch to grow his own fruit and vegetables.

He rather enjoyed working on his vegetable patch and had everything neat and tidy all set out in rows. He had all the fruit bushes at the back of the patch, the marrows and runner beans on one side and rhubarb on the other side. In the centre were lines of carrots, broccoli, onions, cabbage, cauliflower, leeks and beetroot just to name a few.

There is a greenhouse at the side of the vegetable patch where the tomatoes, cucumbers, peppers and seedlings are, they needed to stay to ripen and are doing very well in their little home.

One day after Farmer Betteridge had weeded his vegetable patch a rabbit named Sammy came scurrying along the side of the garden looking for food.

He spotted the vegetable patch and slowly went around so not to catch the eye of Farmer Betteridge or anyone who may be in the garden.

As he approached the patch he heard voices. As he crept closer he saw Clara Carrot talking to Brodie Broccoli. He slowly crept up to them and said "Sorry to interrupt but I need some fresh vegetables for my sister Tia, she isn't very well and my mother wants to make a vegetable broth for her".

"Well you can't have any of us young man" said Clara quite abruptly. "Can't you see we are 'Simply the Best' vegetables you can get and we are only for Farmer Betteridge's table, not for the likes of you".

"But my sister Tia is ill, she got lost in the forest and was out all night and now she has caught a cold, a vegetable broth would help her get better" replied Sammy.

"Well you can't have us, we are far too good for you to eat" said Brodie

"You can have the carrots that have been put in the compost heap which the slugs have had a nibble out of" said Clara.

"Where do you keep your compost heap?" replied Sammy.

"Stanley" shouted Clara. Stanley Carrot came running from the back of the line and coming to a complete halt in front of Clara, stood to attention and saluted.

"Yes Ma'am" he said in a loud voice. "Go and show Sammy where our compost heap is, he wants some vegetables from it to make his sister a vegetable broth" said Clara. "Yes Ma'am" replied Sammy and off he went to the compost heap followed by Sammy Rabbit.

Clara continued her conversation with Brodie saying "Now where were we before we were interrupted, ah yes, we were about to talk about the vegetable competition in the village fete in a few days time".

"Yes I have great expectations from my broccoli florets this year" said Brodie.

"Well I expect to win, with my looks it's in the bag" replied Clara. Then someone from the end line muttered

"More like you will be in the bag with your looks".

"Who said that, own up, I shall find out who said it in the end" Clara raged furiously wafting her foliage back.

Ollie Onion said "Just because you've got good colour, flowing foliage and a loud mouth doesn't mean you will win, we all have as much chance of winning as you".

Clara looked round to where Ollie was sat and said angrily, "You don't have the looks, colour, charm, OR A LOUD MOUTH to even be in the running to win it, so why bother entering the competition". She turned round to face Brodie wafting her foliage with her hand looking totally disgusted at the accusations and ignored Ollie completely.

"Ooh, seems I've ruffled more than a leaf or two there, they say the truth always hurts" remarked Ollie.

Clara pulled herself out of line and walked over to Ollie and said, "No-one would take a second look at you because you have no colour, you're fat and YOU STINK!!!" Then walked back and got in line. She didn't hear another word from Ollie after that.

Later that afternoon Molly and Jack came out into the garden to play tennis, they were having such a lot of fun, so much so that they got a little carried away and the tennis ball went flying into the greenhouse and smashed a window.

"Ouch" said Tommy Tomato "That hurt". "What's wrong" said Connie Cucumber. "Did something hit you?"

"Yes I think it was a ball the children were playing with in the garden and it landed right on my head" replied Tommy.

"Oh no, we're in for it when daddy finds out" cried Molly. "It was an accident, we didn't mean to do it" cried Jack.

They both went to find their father who was milking the cows to tell him what had happened. They weren't looking forward to telling him as his greenhouse was his pride and joy, but it was an accident and they felt sure he would understand.

Meanwhile on the vegetable patch Clara Carrot was bent down on the ground looking quite ill.

"I've been shot Brodie, it's the end for me" she whimpered.

"No you haven't, it was the tennis ball the children were playing with which smashed the window in the greenhouse, that's what made the noise" replied Brodie.

"I thought I was a goner and my beautiful body with a hole in it" remarked Clara.

"You're such a drama queen" remarked Ollie.

In the distance Farmer Betteridge and his children were walking towards the greenhouse to see the damage, Farmer Betteridge did not look happy. As it turned out it was just one small window pane that had broken, much to Farmer Betteridge's delight and could easily be fixed. The children sighed a sigh of relief and continued playing tennis further away from the greenhouse.

Clara being a bit of a bossy boots led the discussion yet again saying, "You can't have a decent conversation without being interrupted all the time with one thing or another, it's just not -ooh, what is that nipping my bottom - ouch!!!"

Clara stood up and looked into the hole she was sitting in and shouted "Who's in there".

Out popped Mr Mole and said "I'm so sorry I nipped you, I must have taken a wrong turning, I do beg your pardon".

"What do I have to do to get a decent conversation around here" Clara shouted out loud.

Mr Mole very quickly made a U turn down the hole and made his way back home.

Brodie and Ollie were crying with laughter, they thought it was so funny, but Clara was not impressed.

A little later Farmer Betteridge came back to the vegetable patch with a basket to gather some vegetables for their evening meal.

"Right everyone stand straight and tall, Farmer Betteridge is going to gather a few of us for his evening meal" said Larry Leek.

"He had better not pick me, I must not be picked till the vegetable competition, there's plenty of other carrots he can pick" Clara replied.

Farmer Betteridge drew nearer and nearer to them and started looking along the lines. "Now which ones shall I pick" he said to himself. "I think I will pick some parsnips with broccoli and carrots" he said quietly.

"What's wrong with cabbage and cauliflower, why doesn't he pick them today" whispered Clara to Brodie.

"Shhh, he's coming closer" whispered Brodie.

He stood in front of the lines looking up and down, holding his chin as if in deep thought.

He bent down and picked up Peter Parsnip and put him gently in his basket.

"Oh my" whispered Clara to Brodie, "That's Peter in the basket, so he won't be in the vegetable competition".

"If he gets any nearer to us neither will we" replied Brodie.

He was just going to bend down to pick a carrot or two when Molly and Jack shouted to their father "There's a phone call from a man about food for the cows for you".

After about 10 minutes he came back out again making his way to the vegetable patch with is basket.

"Now where was I" he said to himself quietly and bent down in front of the lines of vegetables.

He picked Kelly Carrot and Benjamin Broccoli along with some of the other carrots and broccoli florets. He put them in the basket and set off back to the kitchen.

"I really thought he was going to pick us and not have us in the vegetable competition" cried Clara.

"He was getting a bit close, but he is obviously choosing the older vegetables for his table today and saving the younger ones for the competition" said Brodie.

"We will have to start sprucing ourselves up from now on, the competition is only a few days away" said Clara.

"Yes we will have to get some early nights in to make us look fresh and bright" replied Brodie.

"You speak for yourself, I look fresh and bright every morning, I just need a little bit more mascara and lippy on that's all" snapped Clara.

Inside the kitchen Farmer Betteridge gave the basket to his wife and said" This year has been the best ever for my vegetables, I really am torn between which ones are my best for the competition".

Mrs Betteridge replied "These are lovely, I bet they will taste lovely with my roast beef and Yorkshire puddings".

She washed the vegetables then put them in a pan of water. She peeled the parsnips and put them in a tin to roast in the oven. "Look at the size of these parsnips this year, they really are lovely" Mrs Betteridge said to her husband. Peter Parsnip was full of pride and stuck his chest out even more, he loved all the attention he was getting.

The roast beef was already in the oven and smelling absolutely delicious.

Kelly Carrot and Benjamin Broccoli were sat waiting in the pan with the rest of the vegetables waiting for the beef to be cooked a little more before they could get warmed up and ready to be put on the plates.

"How long is this beef going to take, I'm bored" said Kelly.

"You are so impatient Kelly, we'll get going soon enough" replied Benjamin.

Mrs Betteridge started laying the table and getting all the dishes and plates out of the cupboard.

"Oh look she is getting the expensive porcelain dishes out for us, only the best eh!" remarked Kelly.

When the roast beef was cooked along with the parsnips, carrots, broccoli and roast potatoes, Mrs Betteridge put the Yorkshire puddings in the oven then started putting all the vegetables in the porcelain dishes. Kelly and Benjamin felt very special being served in porcelain dishes and were very proud to be on their table.

The dishes were put in the centre of the table along with the roast beef, vegetables, roast potatoes and gravy ready to be served up. When everyone had sat down at the table Farmer Betteridge started carving the roast beef while Mrs Betteridge served the vegetables, Yorkshire puddings and potatoes onto everyone's plates, it smelt delicious.

Molly and Jack said they were not really hungry (they had been eating fruit from the bushes) so not to put too much on their plates, but Mrs Betteridge said "As long as you eat your vegetables and a little meat I don't mind".

"Okay Mummy" the children replied. Farmer Betteridge and his wife had quite a plate full and ate it all up as they were hungry. Molly and Jack seemed to be struggling to finish what was on their plate.

"Come on, eat up" Mrs Betteridge said to them, "then you can have some pudding, we're having Apple Pie today with custard, your favourite".

"I really can't eat the vegetables" explained Jack, and Molly had not eaten much more either.

"Well if you can't eat your vegetables you can't have any room for Apple Pie and custard, so if you really have finished you had better leave the table and Daddy and I will polish off a slice of this lovely Apple Pie" Mrs Betteridge said.

Just at that moment there was a knock at the door. Farmer Betteridge went to the door and was greeted by Farmer Jones from the farm down the road.

"The fence in one of my fields has been knocked down and my sheep are all over the meadow, could I possibly ask for your help with your sheep dogs to round them up please" said Farmer Jones.

In times of trouble all the farmers help one another and Farmer Betteridge had no hesitation in helping Farmer Jones round up the sheep. The children and Mrs Betteridge went to help as well.

Meanwhile on the table Kelly Carrot and Benjamin Broccoli were huddled together hugging one another. "I don't believe we have grown in the vegetable patch for so long and become the very best just to be left on the plate to be thrown away" cried Kelly.

"I never thought it would come to this, oh the shame of it" cried Benjamin.

"We are so good for the children, can't they see we can make them strong and healthy" sobbed Kelly. They were so sad.

After a little while everyone returned from rounding up the sheep. Mrs Betteridge put on the kettle and put the Apple pie and custard on the table. The children looked at the Apple Pie and thought, I'm a bit hungry now after all that exercise rounding up the sheep.

"Mummy" said Molly, "If we eat the rest of our dinner that we left on the plate can we have some Apple Pie and custard, we are quite hungry now".

"Yes of course you can, I'll warm it up for you, I must say I am a little hungry myself after all that exercise" replied Mummy. The children sat down and ate every bit of it and Kelly and Benjamin were so happy.

Mrs Betteridge brought in the Apple Pie and Custard; it looked a smelt delicious and just what was needed to round off a lovely roast dinner.

"Where did you get these apples from Mummy" asked Jack.

"From the apple tree at the edge of the forest, they are lovely big apples there, Granny Smith's I believe. There are loads of apples on that tree, too many to eat as they are, so I thought I would bake an Apple Pie with them as well" replied Mummy.

"Maybe we should go to the apple tree tomorrow and get some more apples" said Molly.

"Well I suppose we could then we can freeze them so we can have apples all winter long" replied Mummy.

"Apples are good for you aren't they Mummy" said Molly.

"Yes they are rich in Vitamin C and are so good for you" replied Mummy.

"When I was little my mother used to say "An apple a day keeps the doctor away" and she always made sure we had plenty of apples to eat" said Mummy.

After dinner they sat down and read a book for a little while, then it was bedtime.

"What are you doing tomorrow Daddy" asked Jack.

"Oh the usual chores around the farm. Why do you want to help me" asked Daddy.

"Well if you want help maybe I can do something for you, but I would like to go with Mummy to get some more apples so we can freeze them as well" replied Jack.

"Okay" said Daddy, "I will think of something for you to do to help after you have been to get some apples, maybe you can help me choose which vegetables I will be entering in the competition in a few days time. This year they are going to judge the vegetables in groups rather than individually which will make a change".

"That will be great" replied Jack.

"We won't be picking them just yet though as I want them to be as fresh as possible but we can at least choose which ones will be in the competition and put a marker next to them so they don't get picked till then" replied Daddy.

Molly and Jack went upstairs and got ready for bed. Mummy and Daddy went into Jack's bedroom first to kiss him goodnight.

"I can't wait for tomorrow to choose the best vegetables" said Jack excitedly.

You get some sleep now, tomorrow is another day.

THE VEGETABLE COMPETITION

Farmer Betteridge got up very early to milk the cows and feed the other animals, then his children Molly and Jack got up and they all sat down to breakfast. They had orange juice with cereals and toast and marmalade. Farmer Betteridge had a cooked breakfast because he had been up for so long he was really hungry. Mrs Betteridge had made him some sausages, bacon and eggs, beans and toast with a cup of tea.

"That's just what the doctor ordered" stated Farmer Betteridge, looking at his breakfast. When you have been up some 3 hours before anyone else you are ready for a good breakfast.

"What time are we going to choose the vegetables for the competition Daddy?" asked Jack.

"I have a few chores to do around the farm first, so if we say after lunch would that be alright"? asked Daddy.

"Yes that is good because we can go down to the apple tree and get some apples to put in the freezer first" explained Jack.

"I need to go into the village to buy a few groceries before I do any apple picking young man" Mummy said.

"Oh can we come with you" asked Molly, "I want to buy some more felt tip pens to do some colouring, my old ones have all dried up and don't work".

"If you want to Molly" replied Mummy.

So after breakfast off they went down to the village. Mrs Betteridge went to the grocery shop while Molly and Jack went to the Post Office and General Stores to look for her felt tip pens. There were lots of different things to buy such as notebooks, colouring books, paints, colouring pencils, felt tip pens. There was so much to choose from she had to have a think about what she would choose.

Jack was looking at the comics on the shelf while Molly decided what she wanted. You shouldn't really read the comics on the shelf unless you are going to buy them, but he had a good excuse in that he was waiting for Molly to choose what she wanted. Mr Penty the Store Manager didn't really mind as long as he was careful.

After a while Mrs Betteridge joined them in the General Store packed up with her groceries.

"Have you chosen your felt tip pens Molly? asked her Mummy.

"There are so many things to choose from I am not sure if I want felt tip pens or colouring pencils, what would you choose Mummy? Molly asked.

"I think the colouring pencils because they won't dry up, all you do with them are sharpen them when they get blunt" replied Mummy.

"The pencils are cheaper than the felt tip pens so can I have a little art book as well please? asked Molly.

"I think that will be alright" Mummy replied. "What do you want Jack, are you choosing a comic? Mummy asked.

"No I think I will go for the felt tip pens and an art book if that is okay? replied Jack. "That is fine, now let's get them paid for and go home" said Mummy.

When they arrived home they had a cup of tea and some biscuits before walking across the field to the edge of the forest to Granny Smith's apple tree to collect some apples.

When they reached the apple tree they looked up and saw a mass of apples on the tree.

"Gosh I have never seen so many apples on one tree" said Molly.

"There are a lot of apples for one tree and we don't want them to go to waste so we will pick some and put them in the freezer. They will last us all through winter till the tree is full again next year. We have the big freezer in the utility room so there is plenty of room for the apples." said Mummy.

"I'll climb up to the top of the tree and get the big ones up there" said Jack.

"No need" said Mummy, "There are plenty we can pick to start with on the lower branches, we can leave them for another day".

Granny Smith looked down to see them picking her prize little ones and she was so thrilled they were going to a good home.

"There you go my little ones, time for you to go" said Granny Smith.

"This is so exciting" said one little apple, "I wonder what I shall be, Apple Crumble, Apple Betty, Apple Pie".

"Whatever you are you will be sweet and delicious and the children will love you, best of all you will make them strong and healthy and in them you will have such adventures together, I am so proud of you all" sighed Granny Smith.

The baskets were getting fuller and fuller and as the apples were put in the basket they would laugh and giggle to one another, they were so excited.

Once all the baskets were full they made their way back home.

The apples were waving goodbye to Granny Smith saying "Thank you for looking after us". Granny Smith had a tear in her eye but she was also very happy and proud of every one of them.

"Goodbye my darlings" she replied.

After lunch Molly and Jack and Farmer Betteridge went up to the vegetable patch so they could choose which vegetables would be entered into the competition. For every one they chose Farmer betteridge would put a little marker stick by the side of them so he would know which ones he would take.

Again Larry Leek was the first person to see them coming across the lawn and said, "Stand by your beds ladies and gents here comes Farmer Betteridge and the children and he's got a basket with him".

"Oh my" said Clara Carrot, "I'm having a hot flush with my nerves being on edge, I tell you Brodie I can't take much more of this, the uncertainty is too much to bear".

"Here we go again the actress coming out, I can't take any more of this" Ollie the Onion said copying Carla's dramatic cries.

"Now, now" said Brodie, "There's no need to be bickering. We will all know very soon now if we are in the competition or not".

"He wouldn't know stardom if it hit him in the face, he has no panache" Clara exclaimed as she threw back her foliage with her hand and turned her back on Ollie.

"Now then" said Farmer Betteridge, "Let's see which ones are the best for the competition, what do you think Molly".

"This cauliflower is lovely and white Daddy, I think this should be in the competition" said Molly.

"Yes it is very white and fresh looking, I think we will put it in as a good contender" said Daddy.

"Look at the Runner Beans Daddy" said Jack, "They are big and long and look very healthy".

"They are also very good for you Jack" explained Daddy. "I think we may have to have a bunch of those to put in the competition, they are in perfect condition at the moment" said Daddy.

"What about some broccoli to go next to the cauliflower on the stand Daddy, it would make the cauliflower look whiter than white and the broccoli look greener than green" explained Molly.

"Yes we could do that and have some carrots on the other side of the cauliflower and a marrow and onions just in front of them, what do think Jack" said Daddy.

"I think it would look good Daddy" Jack said.

They started looking at the broccoli florets. It was so difficult to say which ones were the best as they all looked so good. Brodie was standing to attention with his florets looking fresh and perky. Farmer Betteridge put marker sticks by the side of two of the broccoli further up the line, then slowly walked down the line looking at each one in turn.

He looked at Brodie, then he looked at the one behind him, then back to Brodie, then the one behind him again, then finally he said. "Maybe I should only enter two broccolis as they are good specimens". Brodie was sticking his chest out as far as it would go in the hope of being seen as an even better specimen, but Farmer Betteridge walked away from him. Brodie was distraught. He could not believe that he did not get picked, he felt sure he would be picked.

Farmer Betteridge started looking at the carrots, walking up and down the line looking at each individual carrot for their colour, their green leaves and freshness. Clara was in front of the line looking as fresh as can be making sure her foliage was arrayed properly and looking her best. He stuck marker sticks by four carrots at the back, a couple from the middle of the row and finally coming to the front of the row, he looked Clara over, then looked at the ones he had marked, then back to Clara.

"Yes I think I will mark this one as well, that will make 7 which is a good number" he said.

"Yes, Yes, Yes" said Clara punching her arms in the air, "I've made it.

"Oh I am so sorry you did not make it Brodie, I felt sure you would have done, you are simply the best broccoli here" she said in a sorrowful voice.

"Never mind Clara at least you got in and I'm sure you will go and win it outright" said Brodie.

"Thank you, I'm sure you're right" said Clara smugly, stroking her foliage very confidently.

The children continued on to the parsnips and onions, marking out four or five parsnips and five or six onions, but Ollie was not one of them. Farmer Betteridge and the children then went into the greenhouse to choose some tomatoes and peppers and put markers by the side of them.

"I'm sorry you didn't get chosen Ollie, you are a good looking onion" said Brodie.

"Never mind, I'm sure I'll be appreciated when I'm on the dinner table. I'm sorry you didn't get in too" replied Ollie Onion.

"Oh I'm not that bothered, like you I would much rather be appreciated on the dinner table than stuck in a tent being poked by judges, at least Clara managed to be chosen" said Brodie.

"You might know she would get chosen" said Ollie as he turned to Brodie.

"Yes I am going to be the bell of the ball" chanted Clara in her usual smug voice.

"You want to be careful Clara, you know them slugs are about, if they put a hole in you that's you finished as far as the competition is concerned" said Ollie.

"Where, what do you mean slugs, I can't see any!" Clara cried.

"You never know when they will turn up, they could slither up to you at any time so watch out" said Ollie all eerie like.

Ollie's words made Clara very uneasy and kept a careful eye out for slugs. They normally slither around late at night so Clara kept one eye open as she tried to sleep so they would not get her. She kept nodding off, then waking up, nodding off then waking up till finally she feel fast asleep.

During the night she must have had a nightmare as she woke up with a startle, shouting and waving her hands about, "Get off me, get off me" Clara cried.

"What's wrong with you" said Brodie "There is no-one near you, what is the problem".

"Oh let me catch my breath Brodie" she said gasping. "It must have been a nightmare, I tell you I was in holes, what a mess, I couldn't look myself in the mirror I looked so awful. How could I go into the competition looking like that, it was awful I tell you, awful". Clara was clearly upset by all this, then she remembered who it was who had started all this about slugs · Ollie the Onion!

"It's all your fault Ollie, if you had not said anything about slugs I would have been fine, now look at me, bags under my eyes, and my foliage all crinkled, what a mess I am in, I can't let anyone see me like this" cried Clara.

"All I said was watch out for slugs, how was I to know you would go off in a nightmare about them - a load of fuss about nothing is what I say" explained Ollie Onion.

"Get some sleep now Clara, I'll keep an eye out for you" said Brodie.

"Oh you are kind to me Brodie, you are a true friend - not like Ollie Onion, all he can do is be a nuisance. Yes you are quite right I must get some beauty sleep - Goodnight Brodie" said Clara very sleepily and off she went to sleep.

Brodie kept an eye out for any slugs but eventually fell asleep himself. Ollie Onion had been too annoyed with Clara to sleep so was still awake. As he sat awake waiting for dawn to approach he thought to himself "Maybe I should dip the end of my leaves in that dirty puddle over there and make it look like a slug, then wrap it around Clara's face, she will die of fright in the morning" ha, ha, ha, ha!

Ollie Onion placed the end of his leaf carefully on the side of her face while she was sleeping; it looked just like a real slug. He felt quite pleased with himself, then settled down to sleep.

While he was asleep Brodie Broccoli woke up with a start and thought to himself, "Oh my, I was supposed to be watching out for slugs, I must have fallen asleep". He looked round and saw Clara with what appeared to be a slug on her face.

"Oh dear that looks like a slug on Clara's face" he thought to himself in a bit of a panic. "If I get it off her face she won't know one has been on her when she wakes up" he thought.

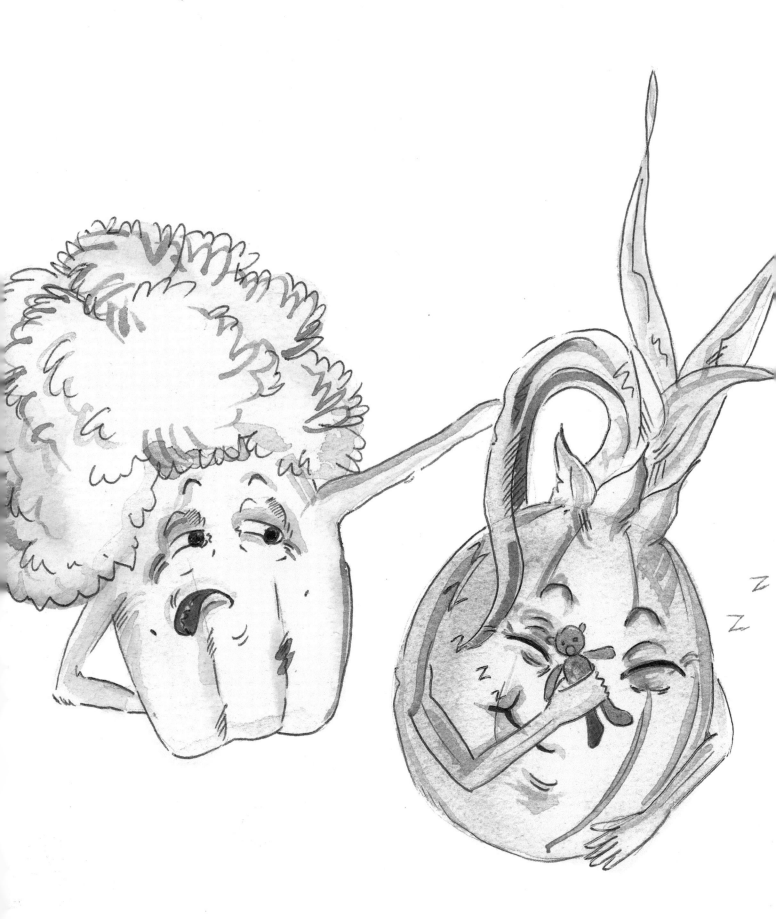

He gently started to remove what he thought was a slug from her face when he saw it wasn't a slug after all but Ollie Onion playing a trick on her, so he thought.

"I know, I will put it on Ollie Onions face instead and when he wakes up he will get the shock not Clara".

He very quietly got out of line and placed the muddy leaf over Ollie Onion's face while he was sleeping, then got back into line.

The next morning Clara woke up feeling refreshed after having a good night's sleep, she looked at Brodie, he was fast asleep. Then she turned around to see the biggest slug on Ollie Onion's face.

She shrieked "Ollie, Ollie, wake up, you've got the biggest slug you ever saw on your face". Ollie Onion woke up quite startled with her loud cries as did Brodie and the rest of the vegetables.

"Get it off Ollie before it puts a hole in you, quickly" cried Clara.

"Where, where is it, I can't see it, get it off me quickly" he said very panicky.

"Don't worry" said Brodie quite calmly, "It won't hurt you".

"How can you say that, you know it puts holes in vegetables, what are you thinking of" cried Ollie Onion, as he wafted his leaves across his face off came the so called slug.

"Where did it go" cried Clara "I don't want it near me, quick find it and get rid of it, put it in the compost heap".

"Don't worry" said Brodie, "Ollie Onion put mud on one of his leaves and placed it on your face to give you a shock, but while he was asleep I put it on his face to give him a shock and I certainly did that" said Brodie, laughing along with all the other vegetables. Clara started to laugh after she realised it wasn't a real slug, but Ollie Onion looked very annoyed that his trick on Clara had backfired onto him and made him look quite silly.

"I'll get you back Brodie Broccoli" he thought to himself.

This trick did actually make them more aware of slugs being around and made sure someone was watching at all times. The big day was drawing near and everyone with markers by the side of them was making sure they looked their best.

"Farmer Betteridge could do with watering us a little more with this lovely warm weather we're having, I'm getting a little thirsty and my foliage could do with a bit of a clean" said Clara.

"Yes it is getting warmer and I am a little thirsty myself" said Brodie.

A little later in the evening Farmer Betteridge came over to the vegetable patch and gave them a really good watering ready for the picking the following morning for the competition.

"Oh that was good" said Clara, "I really needed that, nothing like a good shower to spruce you up and just look how green my leaves are, I'm in tip-top condition, don't you think Brodie"?

"You look just fine Clara, I'm sure you will impress the judges tomorrow" replied Brodie.

The next morning all the vegetables were getting themselves all spruced ready for the competition.

"I can't believe the competition is today Brodie, just think I could be crowned 'Best Vegetable of the Year' that would be a lovely end to the day" Clara said.

A little later Farmer Betteridge and the children came to the vegetable patch to collect his prize vegetables to get them ready for the competition. Clara was one of the first to be put carefully in the basket followed by some of the other vegetables.

Molly was looking at the onion with the marker stick by the side of them.

"Daddy this one without the marker stick looks bigger and better than that one over there with the marker stick" said Molly. Farmer Betteridge came over to have a look.

"Yes you are right it is a better onion and bigger too, we shall have that one instead" he said.

As he put the onion carefully in the basket, Clara looked at him and cried "Ollie, what are you doing in the basket, you weren't picked for the competition."

"It seems I am a bigger and better looking onion than the one he previously chose, so it looks like I am in the competition" said Ollie Onion.

"It's a shame Brodie wasn't picked, he is the best one of the bunch, but still he did not get picked, I feel so sorry for him, he did so want to be in the competition" said Clara.

The basket was getting fuller and fuller, till finally Farmer Betteridge said "I think that's all of them now".

He was just about to walk away when Jack said, "Hold on Daddy you missed this broccoli, it looks better than the one you have in the basket".

"Let me see" said Daddy. "You are right, it does look better and fresher, I think we will have the one in the basket for dinner and put the one you have in the basket for the competition". Farmer Betteridge took the broccoli from the basket and replaced it with the one Jack had. Clara was keen to see who it was and to her surprise and joy it was Brodie.

"Oh I knew you would get in the competition in the end, I just knew it" shouted Clara very excitedly.

"Well who would have thought all 3 of us are in the competition, you, me and Ollie onion" replied Brodie. "Do you think we can all be friends while this competition is on, we all need to pull together as a bunch and be the best we can".

"Yes we must, otherwise we won't win" replied Clara.

"Yes you are right, we must all pull together." said Ollie.

Farmer Betteridge gave the basket to his wife so she could wash them then lay then down to dry and keep cool ready to be transported the next day to the judges' tent.

"I am so excited, I just won't be able to sleep tonight" said Clara excitedly.

"You had better try to sleep or you will look terrible tomorrow and we can sleep safely because there are no slugs in the kitchen" replied Brodie. Eventually they all fell asleep and slept soundly knowing there was no danger of slugs being around.

The next morning Farmer Betteridge gathered them up and put them in a big box with straw at the bottom of it. He gently placed them in his van and off they all went to the judges' tent on the village green.

There were lots of people there and lots of stalls selling just about everything you could think of, it was very exciting for Molly and Jack.

Farmer Betteridge went into the judges' tent with his vegetables while Mrs Betteridge took the children to have a look around the stalls. Farmer Betteridge had given Molly and Jack their spending money so they were eager to see what they could buy.

Farmer Betteridge started to lay out his vegetables ready for inspection by the judges. First he put the cauliflower out, then the big marrow and the leeks in the middle. Below them he put the broccoli including Brodie in front of the cauliflower and the onions including Ollie in front of the marrow. In the centre he put his prize carrots with Clara right in front. What a picture they all looked.

They had all settled down in their right places and put their best front on ready for the judges to inspect them. They were very nervous but quietly confident they would win. "How do I look Brodie" said Clara excitedly.

"You look a picture of health" said Brodie, "And not a slug in sight" looking at Ollie. They all had a little chuckle.

Farmer Betteridge went looking for Mrs Betteridge and the children.

"Ah there you are" spotting them from a distance" he shouted. "What have you bought with your spending money" he said.

"I have bought some clothes for my doll Rosie, she will look lovely in this new dress" said Molly.

"What have you brought Jack" asked Daddy.

"I haven't bought anything yet, but I haven't seen all the stalls yet" said Jack.

Mrs Betteridge bought some homemade jam and chutney and a big chocolate cake for tea.

"They are going to judge the vegetables in 30 minutes time, so we have just got enough time to look at the rest of the stalls and have a quick cup of tea" said Daddy.

So off they went going from one stall to another. Jack bought a toy car and some paints so he could do some painting later that evening and Molly bought a book she quite liked, then they all went back to the tent for the judging of the vegetables.

It was quite a tense moment as there were lots of very good vegetables on the tables. As Farmer Betteridge looked around he could see some bigger and better vegetables than his.

Finally the judges stood in the middle of all the tables to announce the winners.

"You will win!" said Jack.

"I don't know. There are some really fine vegetables on the table this year, I may not" said Farmer Betteridge.

The judges started to read out the winners and had rosettes in their hands waiting to put them beside the winners.

"It has been very difficult to judge a winner this year" said the judge. "They are all so very good, but we have to have a winner so I will place 3rd prize to go to Farmer Harvey, 2nd prize to Farmer Betteridge and 1st prize to Farmer McLaren"

"Oh Daddy you didn't win" said Molly.

"It doesn't matter" said Daddy "We came second which is pretty good considering all the good vegetables on show and anyway it's not the winning that counts, it's the taking part".

"Well done dear" said Mrs Betteridge. "You did very well to come second". Farmer Betteridge went up to collect his rosette and prize which was £30.00 to get more seeds for next year.

Meanwhile Clara was not happy with the result and looked decidedly annoyed.

"I felt we should have won, just look at us all fresh and clean, we should have won!" said Clara.

"It doesn't matter". said Brodie "We've had a good day out and we did come second and best of all we will grace Farmer Betteridge's table tonight, what more could we want?", exclaimed Brodie.

"Well I have to say this is my best day ever and it will be finished off by being on the table with my best friends. We can hold our heads up high as we are simply the best" said Ollie.

Clara looked round to Ollie and said "You are right, we gave it our best and we took part altogether, that's all that matters" said Clara with a smile on her face and they all hugged one another with joy and pride.

When they arrived home Mrs Betteridge made a lovey dinner with all the vegetables and they were proud and happy to be on Farmer Betteridge's table.

"It's been a lovely year" said Clara.

"The best" said Brodie.

"And we are Simply the Best" said Ollie.

THE END.

This book is dedicated to my children Debbie and Michael and grandchildren Ellie, Chloe and Isabella

CPSIA information can be obtained
at www.ICGtesting.com
Printed in the USA
LVIW010721301112

3187LVUK00009B